Little Raccoon's Big Question

By Miriam Schlein

Pictures by Ian Schoenherr

GREENWILLOW BOOKS
An Imprint of HarperCollins*Publishers*

Little Raccoon's Big Question
Text copyright © 2004 by Miriam Schlein
Illustrations copyright © 2004 by Ian Schoenherr
All rights reserved. Manufactured in China
by South China Printing Company, Ltd.
www.harperchildrens.com

Pigment ink and acrylic paint on Strathmore Aquarius II paper
were used to prepare the full-color art.
The text type is 24-point Mrs. Eaves Roman.

Library of Congress Cataloging-in-Publication Data

Schlein, Miriam.
Little Raccoon's big question / by Miriam Schlein ; pictures by Ian Schoenherr.
p. cm.
"Greenwillow Books."
Summary: When Little Raccoon asks his mother when she
loves him the most, she finally answers "always right now."
ISBN 0-06-052116-3 (trade). ISBN 0-06-052117-1 (lib. bdg.)
[1. Mother and child—Fiction. 2. Raccoons—Fiction.] I. Schoenherr, Ian, ill. II. Title.
PZ7.S347 Li 2004 [E]—dc21 2002035328

First Edition 10 9 8 7 6 5 4 3 2

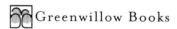 Greenwillow Books

For Timothy and Zoe
—M. S.

For Kathy
—I. S.

"When do you love me most of all?"
said Little Raccoon to his mother.

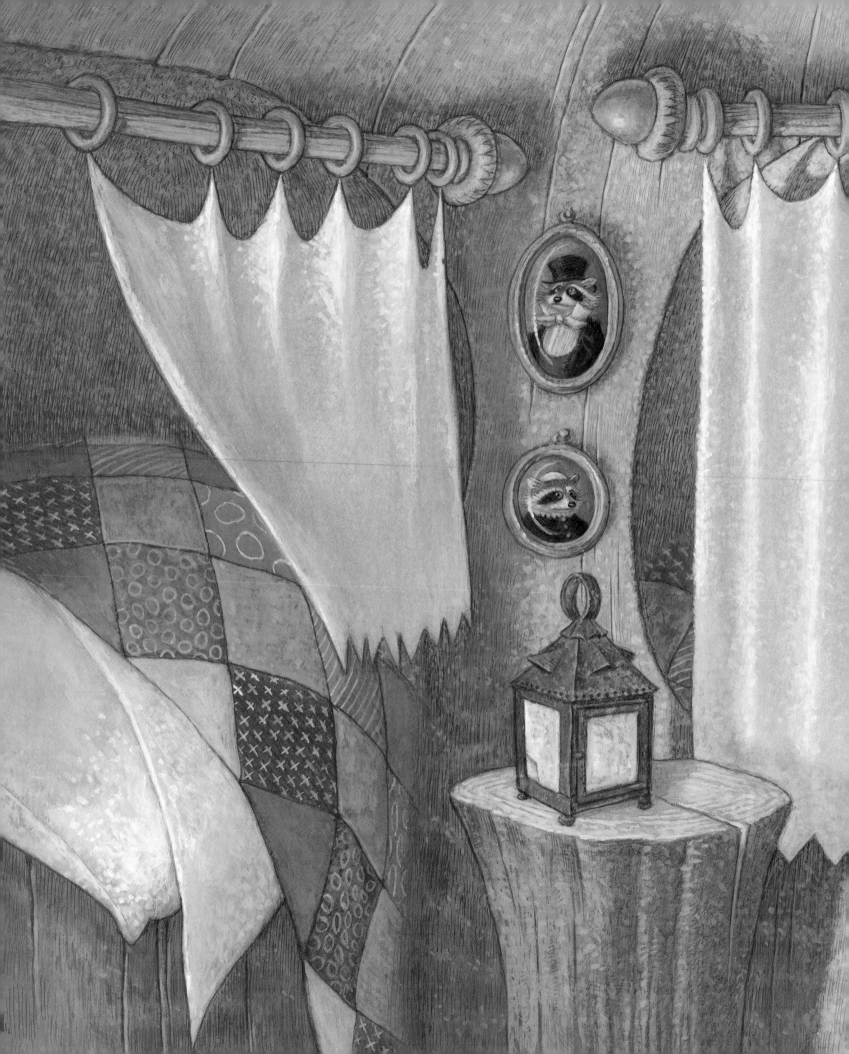

"Is it when I wake up and open my eyes
and poke my nose into your fur?
Is it then?"

"Oh, no," said his mother.
"That's not when I love you most."

"Well . . . let's see,"
said Little Raccoon.

"Is it at feeding time,
when I wash my paws
and wash my food
and am very neat
when I eat?
Is it then?
Is that when?"

"Oh, no," said his mother.
"That's not when I love you most."

"All right,"
said Little Raccoon.

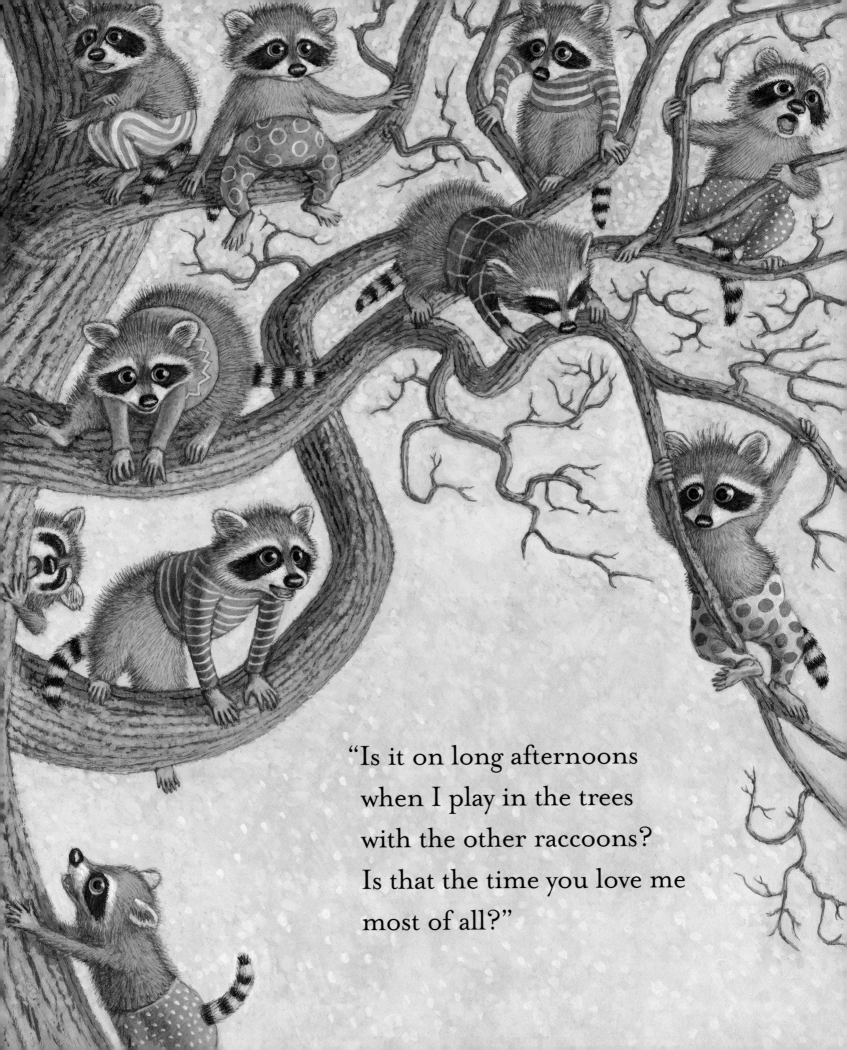

"Is it on long afternoons
when I play in the trees
with the other raccoons?
Is that the time you love me
most of all?"

"Oh, no," said his mother.
"That's not when
    I love you most."

Little Raccoon had to think awhile.

"Okay. Now I know," he said.

"It's when you see
how well I can swim
all the way across the pond
and back again."
He was pretty sure now.
"*That's* when you love me most of all.
It must be then."

"It's true," said his mother.
"You are a *very* good swimmer.
And I *am* proud of you.
But that's not the special time
when I love you most of all."

"Oh."
By now Little Raccoon was
almost running out of ideas.

"Well," he said,
"is it when it's cold,
and we huddle
all close in the den
and peek out
and watch the snow
come down?
Is it then?
It must be then."

"No," said his mother.
"That's not when I love you most."

"When is it, then?" said Little Raccoon.

"It must be sometime.
Is it now, at the end of the day,
when I'm all sleepy and tired?
Oh, it must be now."

His eyes were just about closed.

"Yes," said Mother Raccoon.
"It's now."
She stroked his head.
"NOW is the time
when I love you most of all.
Do you know why?

"Because there is no special time.
I love you *all* the time.
So whatever time of day or night
it happens to be, *that's* the time
I love you most, my little raccoon."

Little Raccoon looked up.
"You mean, right now?"
"Yes, right now," said his mother.
"It's always right now."
   She gave him a little raccoon kiss
   on his little raccoon nose.
   He was so sleepy he almost did not feel it.
   "Oh . . . good," he said.

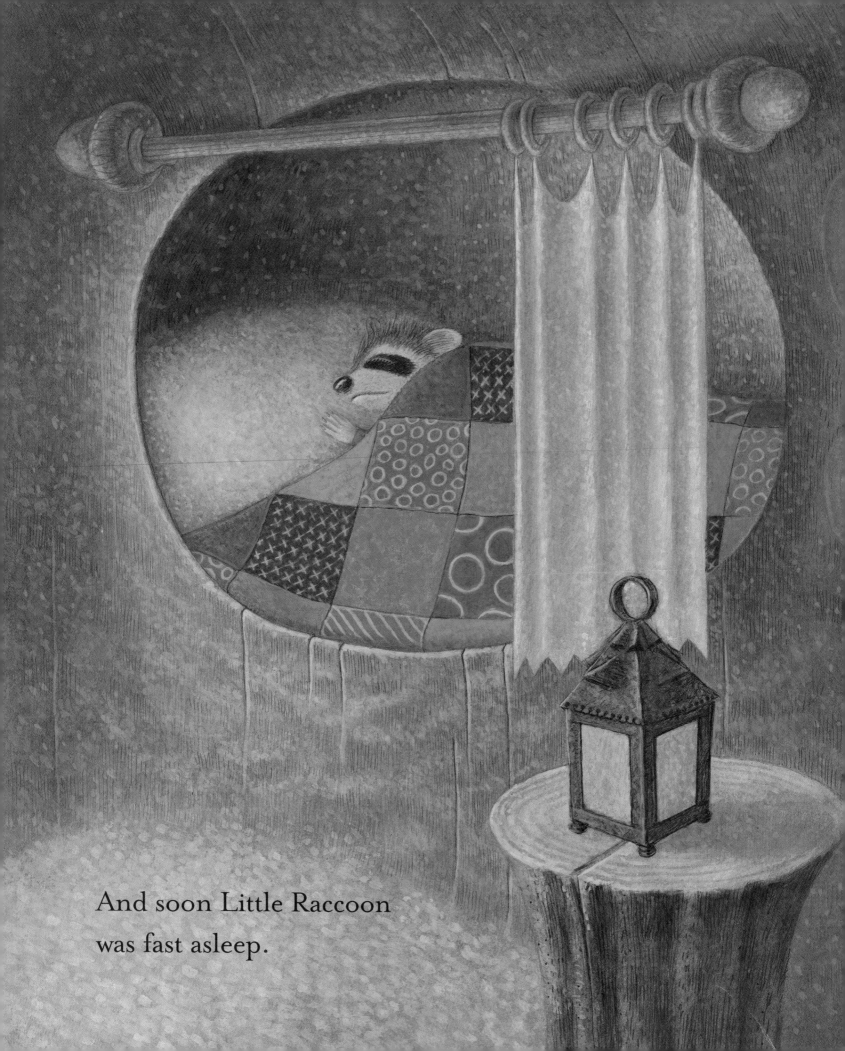

And soon Little Raccoon
was fast asleep.